Shooting Star Stables

by Erin Manson

~ For Bow Belle...RIP ~

Contents

THE CHARACTERS

Callie

Sydney

Lisa

Rea

CHAPTER 1: SHOOTING STAR STABLES

Callie hopped excitedly out of the car, beckoning for her mum, Rea, to hurry up.

"C'mon, Mum! I don't want to be late for my very first horse riding lesson!" said Callie, pulling her mum from the driver's seat.

A lady with dark brown hair came striding towards them, smiling happily.

"Hello! I'm Lisa, the owner. And you must be Callie," said Lisa, smiling at Callie.

"Yep! That's me!" she replied.

The moms exchanged greetings and Lisa pointed to a black-and-white pony's head hanging over the stable door.

"You see that pretty pony? That's Poppy. You'll be riding her today."

Lisa took Callie to the tack room where she helped Callie find a helmet that fitted perfectly. Then they went outside where a girl was leading Poppy over to the arena.

"That's my daughter, Sydney," explained Lisa. Sydney waved. They walked over to the mounting block where Lisa helped Callie up onto Poppy's back, helped her adjust her stirrups and showed her how to hold the reins. Then they set off at a walk around the arena. Lisa made Callie do lots of stretches, but her favourite was when she had to reach forward and touch Poppy's fluffy ears.

When the lesson was over (much to Callie's disappointment), Sydney taught Callie how to groom a horse. After an hour of learning to groom, Callie's mum told her that it was time to go.

"See you next week!" called Lisa as the car drove off.

"You bet!" yelled Callie out the window happily.

She was so excited to come back next week again!

HORSEY WORDS

Tack Room: A room in a stable block that all the horse equipment is kept in.

Arena: A fenced-off rectangle or square in which you ride your horse.

Helmet: A piece of equipment that fits on your head so that you do not hurt yourself when you fall off.

Mounting block: A box or stairs that you climb up to get on your horse's back.

Stirrups: Metal rings in a "D" shape that hang from the saddle and you put your feet in them.

Reins: Long leather straps that you hold onto to steer your horse.

Groom: To brush your horse.

CHAPTER 2: THE PIGLETS

Callie and her mum drove carefully under the sign for Shooting Star Stables, which was threatening to fall down as the wind blew it from side to side.

"My goodness, this wind is harsh!" said Callie's Mum as she parked the car. They ran into the stables just as the rain came down. Lisa was waiting for them, smiling as always.

"Well, hello you," she said, tapping Callie on the nose.

"Today we will earn how to tack up a horse, because it is far too wet to ride."

Lisa led Callie to Poppy's stall where she learned how to tack up. Then she learnt about all the different equipment. There were saddles, bridles, numnahs and a whole lot of other things.

"Right, that's it for…" Lisa was interrupted by Sydney's calls.

"Mum!" she called. "Peggy had her piglets!"

They all ran over to the pig pen, which just happened to be two stables away from Poppy.

When they reached Peggy, ten piglets were lying lazily in the straw.

Peggy

and

her piglets♡

"Would you like to name them?" Lisa asked Callie.

"Me?!" she asked, surprised. Lisa nodded. Callie thought for a bit.

"Okay. That can be Piggy, Porky, Sizzle, Polo, Pirate, Prince, Princess, Romeo and Jessie," said Callie, pointing at each pig as she said their names.

"But there's one left…" said a confused Sydney.

"That's for you to name." smiled Callie.

"Okay! I think I'll call her Rain," said Sydney, beaming from ear to ear.

"I think that's a wonderful name!" said Callie's Mum.

The rain began to stop and all the piglets wandered outside with Peggy, oinking delightedly.

HORSEY WORDS

Saddle: A piece of equipment that sits on a horse's back and is where the rider sits.

Bridle: Numerous straps that fit over a horse's head for control.

Numnah: A piece of cloth that comes in many shapes and colours that goes under a saddle for protection and prettiness.

Stall: A space in which a horse is kept (like a stable).

CHAPTER 3: SHADOW

Callie and Sydney had become such good friends over the past few weeks that they decided to have a SLEEPOVER! Callie packed everything that she was going to need and set off with her mum to the stables.

When they arrived, Lisa was busy teaching someone on Poppy so Sydney was there to greet them.

"Hello! You're going to be riding Winston today. And I'm riding with you!" said Sydney excitedly.

"Really?! How cool!" exclaimed Callie.

The two girls walked over to Winston's stable.

He was a pretty chestnut pony with a long, white blaze.

"Wow! He's so pretty!" said Callie patting Winston.

Winston

The two girls tacked up Winston and went to the arena. They had decided to go on an outride today. Callie hopped onto Winston and Sydney went to fetch Poppy, who had just finished her lesson.

"Be back before 5 o'clock, okay?" called Lisa after them.

"Sure thing, mum!" replied Sydney as the two girls trotted away.

They had been riding for nearly half an hour when they came across an abandoned house.

"Can you hear that?" asked Callie.

"Yes I can," said Sydney, as she faintly heard the barking. "It's coming from the house! Let's investigate."

The girls tied their ponies to a nearby tree and went into the house. The floorboards creaked and shadows lurked in the dark corners.

Suddenly a figure appeared in front of them. It was a black puppy!

"Aww! You poor thing!" crooned Sydney as the puppy began to whine.

"He must be lost. Let's take him back to the stables. He'll be safe there," suggested Callie.

So the two girls left the house and walked slowly back to the farm on their horses, the puppy safely cradled in Sydney's arms.

When they reached the stables, they quickly untacked while the puppy sniffed around the barn.

Then Callie and Sydney took him inside where their moms were talking over a cup of tea.

"Mom!" said Sydney. "We found this puppy in an abandoned house! Look how thin he is!"

Callie put the puppy down and Scruff, the stable's terrier, sniffed him, delighted to have a friend.

Scruff

"Oh my!" exclaimed Lisa and Callie's mum together.

They poured him a bowl of water and got him some food. He began eating straight away.

"Poor thing. We'll have to keep him. We can't just leave him," said Lisa.

"Really?!" asked Sydney.

"Well it wouldn't do any harm. Now, shouldn't we name him?"

"I'll let Callie name him. After all, she was the one who heard him first," smiled Sydney.

Callie smiled back.

"Let's call him Shadow." she said.

"That's perfect!" said Sydney.

Shadow

It WAS perfect. It suited the black puppy. This had been the best sleepover ever! And it wasn't even over yet!

In the morning, the girls fed Shadow and played with him. Then they took him to the barn where Cleo, the cat, didn't even blink an eye. By 11 o'clock Callie's mum was there to pick her up. They said goodbye to Sydney, Lisa and then to Shadow. That was the best sleepover Callie had ever had.

Cleo

HORSEY WORDS

Chestnut: A coat colour that is a mixture of red and brown.

Blaze: A marking that can appear on a horse's face that runs from its forehead to its nose.

Outride: When you take your horse for a walk somewhere other than the arena.

CHAPTER 4: THE NEW PONY

Callie arrived at Shooting Star Stables for her next lesson the following week. Outside the stables stood a horse trailer. Callie found Lisa and Sydney in the stables, tacking up a bay mare Callie hadn't seen before.

"Hello! Who's this?" asked Callie.

"Oh hello!" said Lisa. "This is Rolo. We bought her at an auction today. You are going to be riding her. She seems very sweet."

So the three of them and Callie's mum went to the arena to begin the lesson.

Rolo was a very calm pony but was quite lazy.

They walked and trotted on the lead rein and then Lisa let them ride without the lead rein! So they walked around the arena with Lisa standing in the middle giving instructions.

In the corner, a large bluebird got a fright and flew away. Unfortunately, that scared Rolo. Rolo bolted, trying to get away from the scary bird.

"Sit back! Sit back!" called Lisa, trying to get Rolo to stop. It took a whole three laps around the arena for Rolo to finally calm down and come to a halt.

"Well done for staying on!" praised Lisa. Sydney and Callie's mum were clapping for her on the sidelines. Rolo's ears were pricked towards the noise.

"It was only a bird, silly pony!" chuckled Callie, patting Rolo's neck.

They finished the lesson by walking on a long rein to relax a bit. Then they went back to the stables to give Rolo a nice, long groom.

"Can I ride Rolo next week again?" asked Callie.

"Sure thing!" said Lisa.

Callie couldn't wait until next week!

Rolo

<u>HORSEY WORDS</u>

Bolt: When a horse gets a fright and gallops away.

Bay: A coat colour of a horse. Brown with a black mane and tail.

Mare: A girl horse.

Halt: When a horse comes to a stop.

CHAPTER 5: FIRST FALL

The day of her next lesson, Callie went straight to Rolo's stable, where Lisa and Sydney were waiting for her.

"I'm going to test how well you can put on a saddle and bridle today," smiled Lisa.

So Callie remembered everything she had learnt and did it perfectly!

"Well done!" congratulated Lisa. "Now let's go to the arena. You are going to learn to jump today!"

Callie was super excited! It was finally happening! She was going to learn to jump! She mounted Rolo while Lisa set up some jumps. At first it was just a pole on the ground and Rolo trotted over that easily. Then it got a bit higher. Callie trotted Rolo towards the jump but as the jump loomed ahead, Rolo shied and reared up. Callie lost her grip and flew from the saddle, hitting the ground hard.

She got up almost immediately, still a bit shocked.

"Are you okay?" asked Lisa, her face concerned.

"I'm okay. Is Rolo? Where is she?"

"A true rider!" chuckled Lisa, leading Rolo over to Callie. "Always more concerned about her horse."

Callie got back on and patted Rolo, telling her that there was nothing to be afraid of.

"She has probably never seen a proper jump before," explained Lisa. "We know nothing about her old home."

For the rest of the lesson they worked on getting Rolo used to the jump and at the end they even trotted over it! Callie was so proud of Rolo. When she got off Sydney was by her side.

"Wow!" she said, "That was some fall! Are you okay?"

"I'm fine!" laughed Callie.

The two girls untacked Rolo and played with Shadow, discussing all of Sydney's falls.

Callie really loved Shooting Star Stables and everything she was learning about horses.

HORSEY WORDS

Shied: When a horse moves sideways away from something.

Rear: When a horse moves onto its hind legs, throwing its front legs in the air.

CHAPTER 6: ANGEL

The next week Callie got to Shooting Star Stables just as Lisa was unloading a pretty white foal. She had long legs and a pretty pink nose.

"Oh hello, Callie! Want to come to the arena with me?" asked Lisa when she spotted Callie hopping out of the car.

Callie nodded and followed her, watching as the pretty white foal danced about excitedly.

When they reached the arena Lisa turned around.

"I'm afraid your lesson has been cancelled today." She explained. "Angel here is my friend's foal and she wants me to work with her a bit. Would you like to help?"

"Ooh yes please!" replied Callie excitedly.

They began by making Angel trot around the arena while Lisa explained everything she was doing. Callie got to lead Angel around for Lisa as she called out whether Angel must walk, trot or halt. After about half an hour in the arena, Lisa decided that Callie could take Angel inside the stables and groom her.

"She's so white!" exclaimed Callie as the setting sun shimmered on Angel's back.

"Did you know white horses are actually called 'greys'," said Lisa.

"That's interesting. Why are her legs so dark?" asked Callie, peering down at Angel's knobbly legs.

"That's because all greys are born black. Angel is a Lipizzaner. A very elegant breed. They are known for their excellent dressage movements."

Angel♡

Callie listened as Lisa told her more about the Lipizzaner breed. She tried to remember every little detail. Soon she would be able to get her own horse. Well, maybe.

HORSEY WORDS

Foal: A baby horse.

CHAPTER 7: SUNNY

Callie was thrilled! Today was her birthday and as a special treat, her mum, Lisa and Sydney were taking her to her very first horse auction!

Lisa and Callie's mum sat in the front of the car and Sydney and Callie sat in the back. They were towing a horse trailer just in case Lisa found a suitable horse for the riding school.

They arrived at Blue Diamond Auction House just as they opened the gates. Lisa had insisted that they got there early. While Lisa went to go and get the bidding numbers, Callie, her mum and Sydney looked at all the horses.

Callie helped Sydney make a list of suitable riding school horses. So far it was Razz, Bluey, Skye and Emmy.

"I quite like Skye…" said Sydney. The grey pony had a cute face and was a perfect size.

Skye

"I suppose we should go down to the auction ring now," said Lisa, who had returned from collecting the bidding numbers. Everyone agreed that they had seen what they needed to and made their way towards the ring.

Everywhere was busy with the buzz of people. Time came for them to bid and Lisa was lucky enough to win the bid on Skye!

"Thank you, mum!" said Sydney. Skye was going to be her horse.

"I'll let you ride her every week," said Sydney, noticing the disappointment on Callie's face.

They were about to leave when a pretty palomino entered the ring with a perky trot.

"Ladies and gentlemen, this is Sunny, a super first pony! Anyone bidding on this special guy?" yelled the auctioneer through the loudspeaker.

Lisa noticed the pony immediately. Many people bid on him but Lisa bid higher and higher.

"That's it! Sunny has been sold to bidder 258, Lisa Star!"

When everyone arrived back at Shooting Star Stables, Lisa had birthday cake and presents waiting for Callie. She got a saddle, a bridle and a numnah.

"Thank you, Lisa. But who will I use this on?" questioned Callie.

"On Sunny, of course!" she smiled. "He's your pony!"

"He's mine? REALLY?!" squeaked Callie.

Sunny

"Yep! He's from your mum," explained Sydney.

Callie hugged everyone and ran to the stables to tell Sunny the good news.

He had already settled into his new stable and was munching away at some hay when Callie came up to him.

"Hey, boy! You're going to be my favourite horse in the whole wide world!" said Callie, hugging his pretty palomino face.

This was really the best birthday ever! And it was all thanks to her parents and Shooting Star Stables.

HORSEY WORDS

Palomino: A coat colour of a horse. It is a golden colour with a white mane and tail.

CHAPTER 8: SUMMER VALLEY SHOW

Callie jumped out of the car excitedly and walked towards Sunny's stable. Today was going to be her first lesson on her very own pony!

Callie gave Sunny a mint when she heard Lisa's voice behind her.

"You're here early!" smiled Lisa.

"Just spending some time with my super pony!" said Callie giving Sunny a scratch behind his ears.

"Aah yes. You can go and get his tack and tack him up. I am sure you are ready to handle a pony by yourself. I'll meet you in the arena in 15 minutes." And with that Lisa was off to say goodbye to her other student.

Callie walked into the tack room and smelt the wonderful smell of leather and saddle soap. It was wonderful to see that on one rack there was a saddle and a bridle and on the nameplate it read:

'Sunny: owned and loved by Callie Bloom'

She picked up Sunny's tack and went back to his stable to tack him up. The blue numnah looked amazing on his golden coat. Callie walked him to the arena and noticed that Lisa was busy organising some jumps.

"Callie, come here a minute please," called Lisa.

Callie quickly mounted and trotted over to Lisa.

"I was thinking," said Lisa. "It would be a wonderful experience for you if you did the Summer Valley show jumping competition this Saturday. We could start practising tomorrow?"

"That's awesome! Let's do it!" exclaimed Callie.

"Okay. But for now, let's see how you two get along."

Callie walked, trotted and cantered perfectly. Then she popped Sunny over a few jumps that Lisa had set up.

"You two make a perfect team!" said Lisa walking over to Callie. "I think you two will ace that competition! I also think Sunny deserves lots of carrots. Let's take him back."

So Callie and Lisa took Sunny back to his stable and gave him loads of carrots. Then Callie groomed him, talking to him about the show, and how he is the best pony in the entire world!

CHAPTER 9: IN TRAINING

Callie arrived the next day and was ready to start training. The jumping show was just a few days away! She tacked up quickly and went to the arena. Lisa was there waiting.

"Okay, Callie. Let's just warm him up with some trotting and cantering. Then we can do a few jumps."

Callie nodded and set off at a trot. After the warm up, Lisa told Callie to go over some trotting poles.

"It helps build muscle," explained Lisa.

After the poles, Lisa called Callie towards her.

"Okay," she began, "this is the height you will be jumping in the show." She pointed to a jump that came up to Sunny's chest. Callie was a little nervous. She hadn't jumped that high before.

"So, let's get started. First start at a trot and then canter after the jump to the next one."

Callie did as she was told, but a few strides before the jump she got nervous and pulled up.

"Try again," encouraged Lisa.

So Callie did. This time she didn't pull up but Sunny knocked the pole and Callie lost her stirrups. Sunny began to trot which unseated Callie and she slid to the ground.

"Callie? Are you okay?" asked Lisa.

"Yeah I'm fine, thanks," said Callie, already trying to mount.

"Oh, no you don't," chuckled Lisa. "I think you should have a break. We can practise the morning of the show. I think then when you've seen the jumps it won't be so scary."

"Okay," mumbled Callie and she started to lead Sunny to his stall.

"Well done for trying, Callie!" called Lisa after her, but Callie was deep in thought.

How was she going to ace the show if she couldn't even jump the jumps?

TO BE CONTINUED...

CHAPTER 10: THE SHOW

Callie, Sydney, Lisa and Callie's mum all arrived at Summer Valley Stables at 7:00 a.m. In the horse trailer, Sunny and Skye munched happily away at their hay nets.

Sydney and Callie were going to be taking part in the same class today as it was Sydney and Skye's first show too.

Everyone helped with unloading the horses and then set to work. Lisa had to get the numbers to pin on the girls' riding jackets and Callie's mum had to go and get the riding times and some food. Sydney and Callie had to tack up and groom their horses. Their manes had been plaited earlier that morning. Callie's mum and Lisa came back at the same time.

"Okay everyone," announced Lisa. "Here are your numbers. Sydney, you are rider number 82 and Callie you are 83."

Lisa pinned the numbers onto the girls' show jackets.

"And I have some bad news," said Callie's mum.

"What?!" said everyone in unison.

"Callie, you are riding in 10 minutes."

"What?!" cried Callie. "But I need to practise!"

"New plan," said Lisa, "Callie, you're an excellent rider. Your pony is a master at this stuff. You just go into that arena with a steady mind and you will be amazing!"

Just then the judge made an announcement.

"Rider number 83, Callie Bloom on Sunny, you are needed on standby at the arena."

Lisa gave Callie a leg up and wished her luck.

"Okay boy," Callie whispered into Sunny's ears. "This is it. I know we can do this. The best pony in the world can do anything. Let's go have some fun."

Callie patted his neck and the bell rang to start her round. She urged Sunny into a canter and off they went. As the first jump loomed ahead, Callie felt the butterflies dancing in her stomach. She put her leg on and closed her eyes.

1, 2, 3... hup!

They had made it over!

The rest of the round Callie had full confidence in Sunny. The final jump came and went. Clear round! The audience burst into applause. Callie hugged Sunny hard and the proud pony held his head high and whinnied.

"Well done!" said Lisa.

"You were amazing!" said her mum.

"Totally!" grinned Sydney.

Sydney came back from her round a little while later.

"How did it go?" asked Callie.

"I knocked a pole," explained Sydney. "But other than that Skye was amazing!"

"Well girls, I am very proud of both of you. You were both amazing!" said Lisa. But she was interrupted by the judge announcing the winners.

"Right," began the judge. "In third place, we have Clara Flock on Wendy."

The crowd applauded and a girl came trotting into the arena on a pretty bay pony.

"In second place, we have Sydney Star on Skye!"

Sydney looked so surprised and kissed Skye and trotted into the arena to collect her blue rosette.

"And in first place... Callie Bloom riding Sunny!"

Callie hugged Sunny.

"We did it, boy!" she laughed.

She trotted to the arena to claim her beautiful red rosette. Then the three winners did a lap of honour. And while Callie was cantering around, red ribbon streaming from Sunny's mane, she realised that she could never be prouder. She came first! And it was all thanks to her super pony!

~ Thank you for reading ~

ABOUT THE AUTHOR

Erin Manson is 13 years old and has ridden horses since she was 8. Shooting Star Stables is her first book and she hopes to write many more stories about girls who love horses and get to experience the joy of owning one of these wonderful animals.

Printed in Great Britain
by Amazon